Beyond Blind Faith

Beyond Blind Faith

A Thinking Person's Guide to Meaning and Inner Peace

David Naggar

DaJé Publishing

BEYOND BLIND FAITH:
A Thinking Person's Guide to Meaning and Inner Peace
 First Edition

ISBN 1-57746-560-1

Library of Congress Catalog Number: 99-90322

Book design: Marc-Pierre Sanchis
Cover design: Roger Dawson & John Rafferty
Cover Image: Images® copyright 1999 PhotoDisc, Inc.

Published by DaJé Publishing,
1824 Beach Street, San Francisco, CA 94123.

Printed in the U.S.A.

Acknowledgements

I would like to acknowledge the thoughtful and generous assistance I've received from Rebecca Cleff, Roger Dawson, Mary Beth Grabon, Susan Heller, Molly Maguire, Maile Melkonian, Avner Naggar, Anna Nelson, John Rafferty, Marc-Pierre Sanchis and Aaron Silverman.

I'd like to give special thanks to Vivian Alberts, who graciously read and commented on many draft manuscripts; to Auri Naggar, whose extraordinary intellect and insight were always available to me; and to Norm Coleman and Tamra Donovan, who not only read and commented on multiple draft manuscripts, but did so with great acuity, patience, and dedication. Their support has been invaluable.

Contents

The Search for Answers

Throughout time and across every culture, people have shared the need to experience spiritual meaning. As part of the search, people have been asking, debating and giving answers to the following questions for thousands of years.

Where does the universe come from? Does God exist? Is there a plan or meaning behind all that happens? Is the universe divided into good and evil?

We have also searched for answers about our role in the universe. Who are we? How is it that we are capable of asking questions? Why are we here? Where are we going? Do we have a soul? Is there salvation? Is there life after death?

And we have sought knowledge about our humanity. Which part of our character are we born with, and which part is learned after we are born? What is human nature? Is right and wrong the same for everyone? How should we treat each other? How should we live in order to live a good life? How do we find inner peace?

Our attempt to answer these questions can be compared (much in the same way Albert Einstein attempted to explain our understanding of reality) to a person trying to understand the mechanism which operates inside a sealed pocket watch. A person studying the watch can observe the hands of the watch move and hear the watch tick, but has no way of opening the case. A creative person may form a mental picture of the mechanism responsible for the ticking and the moving hands but the person can never be quite sure if the image is the true explanation. If the case remains unopened, the person can never actually compare his or her explanation with the real mechanism.

The quest for spiritual meaning calls us to understand the mechanism of our lives.

Fundamentalists of most sects have argued that their particular answers offer the only Truth. This has never made much sense to me. I believe that behind the differing metaphors, each sect is trying to explain the same wonder, a wonder which is ultimately still a mystery. Like the metaphor of Einstein's watch, no one is able to know for certain if his or her explanation matches reality. The proof to support any particular answer is elusive without making assumptions. That is why if you believe an answer is true, you have made a leap of faith. But the leaps you choose to make needn't be arrived at blindly.

If you do not experience meaning and inner peace, look first to your current answers, that is, the beliefs you hold and the leaps of faith which underlie them. These beliefs shape your core—the core from which all else about you flows.

Like the first domino which causes other dominoes to fall in turn, your beliefs guide your other thoughts *and* your actions. They affect everything about you—your self esteem, how you interact with others, your ability to live in peace.

Certain beliefs are more likely to lead you toward meaning and peace than others. And some beliefs will not lead you toward meaning and peace, even if the actions you take in life reflect them. Perhaps you have unknowingly made an assumption which has led you to adopt a negative belief—one which does not lead you toward spiritual meaning and inner peace. As an obvious example, if you have a belief that people at their core are truly selfish, and you treat everyone accordingly, you are bound to be miserable, and are not likely to experience peace.

This is why you must examine the sources of your deepest beliefs, and the assumptions and leaps of faith which underlie them. How did you arrive at your answers? How did your parents and other childhood care givers arrive at their answers?—Answers which they have most likely imparted to you.

I wrote this book to stimulate your personal search, as well as my continuing search, for answers. It is my hope that it will be a spark which leads you toward spiritual meaning and inner peace—the seeds of a life lived in harmony with yourself and others.

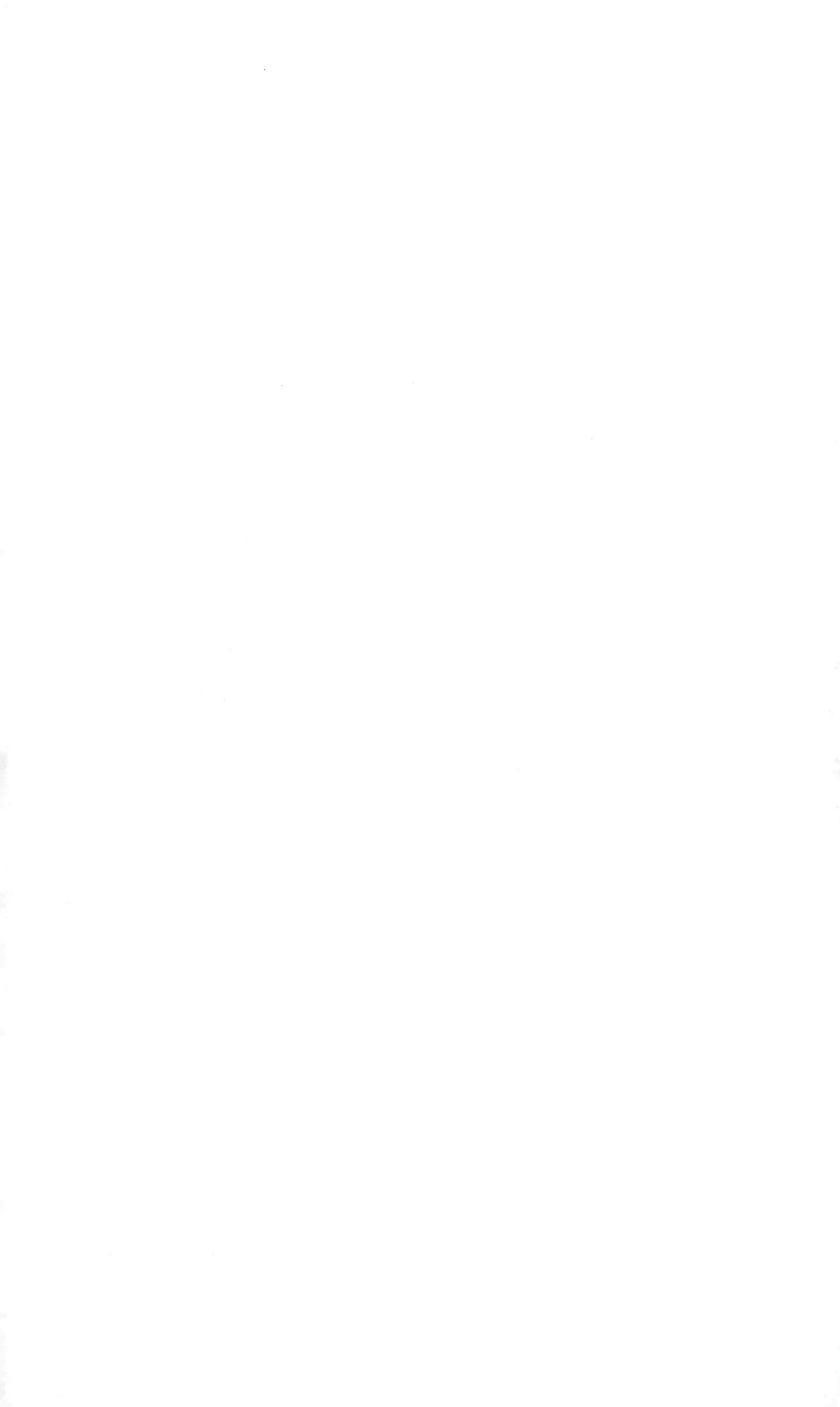

PART I

Explorations

Community-Influenced Beliefs

If you trace the origins of your deepest beliefs, you will likely find that most of them are derived from the story of humanity passed down through the generations—the story told in your community.

Throughout history, *every* community has told the story of humanity because people have the need to tell and understand the human story.

Though each community (whether a national or religious community) has its own version, the underlying purpose of each story is the same; to answer questions about the unknown forces of the universe; to answer questions about human existence.

Every community tells of the journey of a person's life—from birth (arrival) through dependency, adulthood, maturity, and finally, through death (departure). Each story is told to help a person better experience the essence of being alive, understand who he or she is, appreciate the unknown, and touch the eternal.

Through these narratives, each community's underlying assumptions about existence, humanity, and expected personal behavior is revealed. Each community offers its own image of the mechanism which operates inside the sealed pocket watch.

Often these stories are not meant to be taken literally. They may contain symbolic representations of ideas and principles that are difficult to share precisely through words. Words, after all, are only one form of communication, and the human mind is filled with thoughts which cannot be easily expressed in words. Through symbolism, a person is beckoned to transcend the visible, and reach toward understanding matters which are beyond words.

But if this transcendence is to occur, a community's stories must reflect the world of its time and place. If transcendence does not happen, the stories will be intuitively discarded as irrelevant by its people. They will not serve to enlighten anyone.

Today, world population has exploded. Communities which once contained thousands of people are now comprised of millions. They have become large and impersonal.

Material prosperity and technological advances have dramatically altered our daily experience from the daily experience which was known to people who lived in centuries gone by. And because this has happened within the span of only a few generations, most communities have not dealt well with our need to tell and understand the story of existence, the story of life, and the story of humanity in terms of the world we live in today. Communities continue to tell stories of life which were offered in another era, and from a different life experience.

That is why each successive generation discards more and more. And each generation renews the natural search for meaning and inner peace which speaks to them. A meaningful story of humanity must be told; the void must be filled.

My point is this: Not all stories of life which were told by ancient nomadic tribes and agricultural communities are suited to guide your life. Those stories were told to be meaningful for that time and place. (For example, should we really continue to be fruitful and multiply, if in the process we overburden the ability of the planet to sustain us?)

While a great deal can be learned from the past, a great deal of unhappiness can result from continually guiding your life and your actions by the beliefs (and the underlying assumptions) of people who lived in a different era.

Roots ⌣

Many beliefs taught in communities throughout the world share common roots.

There is a certain pride we each feel about our unique roots. But in reality, your roots are not as unique as you might think. Ancient civilizations borrowed from each other once contact was made. Current civilizations adopt ideas from each other still.

The languages of most European nations and most Indian and Iranian languages share a common root; a root which derives from tribes who lived between the Black Sea and the Caspian Sea two thousand years before the birth of Jesus. These Indo-European people journeyed in all directions and became integrated into local cultures spanning from England to India. This likely explains the similarity of the early myths told in these different cultures.

Judaism, Christianity and Islam share a common Semitic root. The Jewish Torah and the Muslim Koran were both first written in the Semitic family of languages.

The early Semites believed in one God and viewed history as progressing from a beginning to an end. In the beginning God created—that was the beginning of history; one day, history will end—this will be the Judgment Day, the day on which God judges all people, living or dead. This perspective of the early Semites is still the perspective of many people today.

The New Testament is, in essence, Christianity's supplement to the Jewish Bible. But it was first written in Greek. It is therefore not surprising that Christian theology takes from both its Semitic roots and from Greek (Hellenistic) tradition.

The medieval Christian philosopher St. Augustine, who lived from 354-430, believed in the Semitic tradition which held that God created the world from a void. Yet he made a great effort to explain the philosophy of Plato so that it conformed with Christianity.

Likewise, the medieval Christian philosopher St. Thomas Aquinas, who lived from 1225-1274, made a great effort to explain the philosophy of Aristotle so that it conformed with Christianity.

Historically, western religions emphasized a duality, that is, a separation between God and God's creation (God in heaven, people on earth). A purpose in Christianity is for people to be redeemed by God from sin and fault.

It was St. Augustine who argued that the biblical fall from grace in the Garden of Eden meant that all humans are the seeds of the original sin, and that no man is actually deserving of God's redemption. St. Augustine also said that only by the grace of God are some chosen to be saved from damnation. (A belief in this view of original sin may lead some people to think poorly of themselves; it may also lead some to be more forgiving of others.)

Eastern religions such as Buddhism and Hinduism center on a monistic view of deity and creation; that is, a view that everything is one, and that the presence of the deity is in all things.

This view helps to explain why in the Far East, seclusion and passiveness come easily for many. One who believes in the presence of the deity in all things is more likely to lead a more compliant existence. The need to dominate surroundings is minimized if one accepts that he or she is a part of it. It seems natural that this belief will lead to the practice of self-introspection and meditation.

Yet this Eastern way of life is not historically isolated from the Western tradition. In ancient Greece & Rome many people also believed religious seclusion was the way to find the salvation of the soul. Plotinus, a Roman philosopher, who lived from 205 to 270, also believed that God is present in all things. In fact, many aspects of medieval Christian monastic life derive from this view of humanity's relationship to God and existence.

Today, this ancient world view, which is now often considered Eastern, is held by a growing number of people in the West, irrespective of their stated religious denomination.

And so, a lesson which can be learned from our roots is this: The roots of Western thought and Eastern thought, are bound both to ancient philosophy, and to each other. Try to look beyond your immediate community for your answers. Consider the possibility that all of humanity is your community from which you can draw wisdom.

Greek Philosophy

The conflicting beliefs of ancient Greek philosophers (Hellenistic period) have had a great influence on the common threads of deep spiritual thinking. You will likely see reflections of some of your beliefs in them.

Before the Hellenistic period, Greeks, Romans, Persians, Babylonians, and Egyptians worshiped their own deities. Teachings about salvation from death flourished, and believers were promised eternal life and immortality of the soul if they embraced certain teachings, and performed particular rituals.

Through the Greek conquests of Alexander the Great, these cultures and their creeds began to merge. It was during this time that the walls between religion and philosophy were torn down (only to be rebuilt in the Renaissance period).

The ancient Greek philosophers posed many questions which are still being posed today. They wondered: Are there natural, rather than supernatural reasons which explain what we see around us? To the philosophers it became unacceptable to explain that a war was lost because of the vengeance of a deity. Compare the Greek thinking of the time (between 400 and 500 B.C.) to the thoughts contained in the Old Testament. The Old Testament attributes lost wars to God's anger with the people.

And early Greek philosophers theorized that everything that exists always existed, and that there had to be an invisible root that was the source of all the things that they knew. They debated the nature of the source, and how it was able to reconstruct itself to appear to be different material things, such as a stone or a living being; but they rejected the notion that the trials and tribulations of fighting gods explained their world. Rainfall became natural, and seasons became natural, and helplessness began to give way. Humanity grew.

And they wondered: Is what we perceive of the world through our senses of sight, hearing, taste, smell and touch reliable?

Parmenides was born circa 515 B.C. He thought that there could be no such thing as actual change because he believed that the root source of everything —whatever it was—was constant and unchangeable. Yet, to his human senses, it appeared that nature was constantly changing; wood burned to ashes, and winter looked different than spring. He therefore thought that people's ability to reason with the mind must be more reliable than people's sensory experiences.

Heraclitus, who lived at about the same time as Parmenides, thought that the fact that everything was in a constant flux was the most fundamental attribute of nature. He believed that human sensory perceptions were reliable.

Empedocles lived circa 495 to 435 B.C. He tried to fuse Parmenides' and Heraclitus' views. He theorized that although nothing changes (Parmenides), human sensory perceptions were, nonetheless, reliable (Heraclitus). To arrive at this conclusion, he challenged one of the accepted assumptions of both schools; he concluded that there had to be more than one basic root substance. He suggested that there were four; earth, air, fire and water. He then argued that the changes in nature that people saw were due to the coming together and separation of these four substances.

While basic chemistry long ago established that Empedocles' speculation was wrong (there are many elements, not four root substances), the foundation was laid for many practices which are still performed by some today. For instance, the twelve signs of the horoscope are still classified as earth, air, fire or water signs.

Democritus lived circa 460 to 370 B.C. He thought that since the changes seen in nature could not be due to the fact that anything actually changed, everything must be composed of minute invisible particles; particles which he called atoms. He therefore concluded that nature consisted of a limitless number and shapes of atoms, which could join together in such a way as to create the variety of things we see.

Democritus also thought that each atom was eternal. He theorized that when a thing actually died, the atoms moved on and formed a new thing. He thus concluded that there could be no life after death, because when we die, the "soul atoms" disperse in all directions.

And Greek philosophers also wondered: What part of human behavior are we born with, and what part is caused by our environment?

The renowned Socrates, who lived from 469 to 399 B.C., was reported to have said "I know that I know nothing." He argued that although we have our five senses and our reason to guide us, none of us can be certain of what we know. Yet he is also said to have believed that there is a universal right and wrong which we possess at birth without need of experience.

When Socrates lived in Athens, he lived alongside philosophers called Sophists who thought it was a waste of time to speculate on philosophical questions regarding human nature and the universe. Sophists did not deny the possibility of answers, they simply believed that humans could not know them. They did not believe in the existence of absolute norms which could be used to distinguish right from wrong.

Plato, who lived circa 427 to 347 B.C., believed that we possess only a partial understanding of what we perceive with our senses, but that we can possess true knowledge of what we understand through our reason.

Plato focused on the interaction between what he considered to be eternally unchangeable (in nature, and regarding morality), and what he considered to vary (not subject to absolute universal norms or truth).

He believed that everything tangible is made of a material which time wears away, but that everything material originates from a timeless "pattern" or "form" that is eternal and unchangeable.

Plato compared the tangible phenomena that we see as akin to shadows of the eternal forms. He thought that everything in the material world is an imperfect copy of its eternal form. The mold itself (the eternal form) is always perfect, but whatever is made from the mold is always less than an exact copy. There is a mold for a man and a mold for a horse, but there is no mold for a cross between a man and a horse. This is why Plato concluded that we do not see any.

While genetic engineering proves Plato wrong, it is Plato who lays a foundation for many to divide our being into two: a split between the perfect and timeless soul (what he called the idea world), and the body (what he called the material world).

Plato also believed that the soul exists before residing in the body, and wants to ultimately be free of the body. He has truly influenced the thinking of the generations that have come after him. If a person is presumed to possess an immortal soul, the soul must operate more or less independently from the body because we know that our bodies wear out. This presumption has great theological consequences.

Aristotle lived from 384 to 322 B.C. and was Plato's student. He is considered by many to be the founder of the science of logic. He was also a master organizer who classified a thing by what it could or could not do. Aristotle divided non-living things from living things. He subdivided the living things into creatures and plants. He then subdivided creatures into animals and humans. Aristotle placed humans at the top of the chart (other than God), because humans, he said, are capable of doing more than other living things; we grow, as do plants and animals, we move and perceive, as do animals, but on top of this, we alone are capable of rational thought, the spark of divine reason.

To Aristotle, what we perceive with our senses is as real as reality could be. He viewed the question of whether the soul and the body are one (Democritus) or two (Plato) as presenting a false choice, like an attempt to separate sight and the eye. To Aristotle, the soul is the set of capabilities which occur through our physical nature. He viewed the soul as a reflection of our physical world.

Cynics were Greek philosophers who believed that true happiness is not found in things such as material wealth, power or good health. To Cynics, true happiness is achieved by being free of dependence on such arbitrary and temporary things, and by pursuing a life of virtue for its own sake. They therefore concluded that happiness was possible for everyone, and that once attained, happiness could never be lost.

Stoics were Greek philosophers who believed that the cosmos is alive and rational, and that the universe is one organism without separation. They believed that each person is a miniature reflection of the whole of the cosmos. Stoics were monists, not dualists (that is, they believed in one nature, and not a separation of nature between spirit and matter). They believed that nothing happens by accident, that all is destined, and that fate should be accepted without complaint.

Skeptics were Greek philosophers who believed that anyone who believed he or she could know reality was bound to be continuously frustrated and unhappy. They believed that people who truly set aside judgment and recognized that their beliefs about reality were not necessarily valid would achieve peace.

Epicureans were Greek philosophers who believed that pleasure was the starting point of a good life. They believed that the goal of life was to achieve the maximum amount of sensory enjoyment, and to avoid pain and worry. In order to avoid ultimate suffering and anxiety, Epicureans believed that people needed to overcome the fear of death. They thought that as long as a person exists, death is not present; and when a person dies, human "soul atoms" simply disperse (like Democritus). Since humans no longer exist in death, Epicureans said that there was simply no disturbance in being dead. They concluded that because death was not to be feared, the gods were not to be feared.

And so, beyond seeing the seeds of some of your beliefs in the differing ancient Greek philosophies, a lesson which I hope is reinforced is this: To believe—actually, to live—requires faith of one kind or another. Reliance on faith, that is, the inability to prove the truth of a particular answer once and for all, is the reason we continue to pose many of the same questions over and over again in each generation.

Philosophy is a study that is best at posing questions, not at providing definitive answers to them.

By posing great questions, whether or not you eventually arrive at definitive answers, your mind expands.

Later Philosophy

More recent answers to the same questions posed by the Greeks and other early philosophers have also greatly influenced spiritual thinking.

In the last few years before the birth of Jesus, the Roman empire began to supplant the Greek empire.

Plotinus, the Roman philosopher who lived from 205 to 270, believed in the dual nature of man: a body made of the substances of the material world, and an immortal soul. Plotinus also theorized that evil was outside the realm of what he called the One. He thought that thinking otherwise would be thinking meanly of the One.

Recall that St. Augustine lived from 354 to 430. He was the very influential Christian theologian who argued that we are all sinners because Adam disobeyed God and ate from the tree of knowledge.

During the Renaissance period, which began in the late 14th century, Europeans began to view themselves less as sinful beings and more as worthwhile beings. Technological revolution was everywhere—the magnetic compass permitted navigation of the globe and led to more accurate readings of star and planetary positions, the advent of the mechanical clock changed people's view of time, and the printing press allowed for the dissemination of widespread knowledge.

Because the Protestant movement and the Catholic Church of that day denounced scientific discoveries which contradicted the literal truth of passages in the Bible (it was considered an affront to God to suggest that the sun did not revolve around the earth), the study of philosophy began to be viewed as different than the study of religion. As people began to have more credence in scientific discovery, the idea that life is solely a preparation for the afterworld was supplanted by a new way of thinking about everything earthly.

René Descartes lived from 1596 to 1650. He is considered by many to be the father of modern philosophy, and his thoughts are still highly influential today. It is Descartes who said, "I think, therefore I am." He said this because he was certain that he was able to doubt, and in order to doubt, he had to be thinking. He therefore concluded that it had to be true that he actually existed, and was a thinking being.

Descartes was also concerned with the relation between mind and body. He believed that spirit and matter were completely separate, yet he searched to understand how something non-material (the spirit in the mind), could influence the physical body and start a process that is mechanical.

God's existence was self-evident to Descartes because he could conceive of a perfect entity, even though he himself was not perfect. He felt that a non-perfect entity could not conceive of a perfect entity unless the idea of a perfect entity originated elsewhere, that is, with the perfect entity.

Observe that the seeds of Descartes' philosophy were planted by Plato and his idea of perfect forms. Similar arguments are still advanced today in order to establish the existence of God.

Baruch Spinoza lived from 1632 to 1677. He was excommunicated as a Jew because his own historical review led him to conclude that God did not inspire every word of the Bible. Spinoza theorized that God is everything that exists, and that everything that we know to exist is a part of God. In other words, Spinoza believed that there is really only one substance, and that everything is part of it; a monistic view, not a dualistic one.

Descartes and Spinoza are often called Rationalists because they contended that the main source of knowledge is innate ideas; that is, ideas we are born with—ideas which exist in the mind before we have experiences.

Thomas Hobbes who lived from 1588 to 1679 is often called a Materialist. He believed that reality—all things *and* thoughts—is entirely dependent on matter. He theorized that human consciousness emanates from the movement of matter in the brain.

Philosophers called Idealists contended that nothing is real except minds and their ideas. They believe that all material matter which we perceive to exit must be ultimately spiritual in nature.

John Locke lived from 1632 to 1704. David Hume lived from 1711 to 1776. They are often called Empiricists because they contended that nothing could exist in our minds that had not been first experienced through our senses. Observe how different this view is from the view of Descartes and Spinoza who state that our ideas are innate, and so, preexist our experience.

Observe also that the philosophy of Locke and Hume is traceable to Aristotle. It was Aristotle who said that nothing exists in our consciousness which has not been first experienced by our senses. And it was Aristotle who said that none of us has ideas that are independent from his or her senses, even though each of us possesses an inborn power of reason, and an ability to organize our sensory impressions.

The Age of Enlightenment (mid to late 18th century) produced many philosophers who believed that each person must find his or her own answers to every philosophical question, and that each person can do so through reason. Yet they believed that faith in God, and the ability to distinguish right from wrong, were an inborn part of the human ability to reason.

Immanuel Kant lived from 1724 to 1804. He suggested that both our inborn reason and our senses contribute to what we can know about the universe. He believed that the world does not exist entirely as we perceive it because we experience things through senses which conform to our human physical makeup. He also concluded that we can never reason our way to absolute certainty about the answers to great metaphysical questions such as the existence of God, immortality, or our free will because even when we reason, we do it from within the limits of a human perspective.

Kant thought that it is our innate reason which causes us to distinguish right from wrong. Compare this view to Hume's theory. Hume thought it is our feelings which cause us to distinguish right from wrong.

Georg Hegel lived from 1770 to 1831. Most philosophers who came before Hegel attempted to identify what humanity could know about the universe by assuming the timelessness of humanity's knowledge of the universe. A human was a human, and most philosophers and philosophies seemed to allow for no growth. Hegel believed that human understanding evolves with each succeeding generation. He did not believe in the existence of eternal truths, which could be derived from timeless reason, because he questioned whether any philosopher, or any thought, could be detached from that philosopher's historical context.

Karl Marx lived from 1818 to 1883. He believed that what a society considers moral depends in part upon economic material factors such as the type of goods it produced, the means used to produce them, and who owns the means of production. He also believed that there is a strong link between the work a person does and the way he or she thinks.

Sigmund Freud lived from 1856 to 1939. He argued that we are not as rational as some philosophers suggest. Freud believed that human actions are not always guided by reason. He argued that irrational urges often shape not only what we do, but what we think. Yet, in essence, Freud is merely analyzing the human brain from a different perspective than other philosophers. His separation of the brain into the Id, the Ego and the Superego is his attempt to explain our minds and our behavior.

Jean-Paul Sartre lived from 1905 to 1980. He theorized that a person does not possess an innate human nature, and must therefore generate his or her own. Because of this belief, like the Sophists of ancient Greece, Sartre concluded that it was pointless to search for the definitive meaning of life. He believed that each of us must find his or her own meaning and decide how to live best.

Philosophy goes round and round. The logical proofs which are offered, though detailed in the extreme, still rest on assumptions of one kind or another.

Observe that many broad principals of new-age philosophies can be found in the thinking of the Greek Stoics (the cosmos is alive and rational; the universe is one organism without separation).

And the Christian description of God as the non-material source of the world (though not responsible for the evil seen in the world), is the description Plotinus used to describe what he called the One.

And the Christian belief in the separation of body from soul, is the same separation argued by Plato.

Now, occasionally a long-debated philosophical point is settled because something new is learned. It is then said to belong to a realm other than philosophy.

Democritus' conjectures about the different structures of atoms have been shown to be wrong, and the study of atoms is no longer in the realm of philosophy; it now belongs in the realm of physics and chemistry. Yet Democritus' philosophic conclusions are still debated. Is there life after death? Do we have a soul?

You see, even philosophers who are acknowledged to be the greatest of human thinkers, assumed things which have been proven wrong. Yet by posing great questions, they have helped expand our minds.

Philosophical Questions

The philosophical questions themselves greatly influence spiritual thinking.

Hobbes and Freud were merely seeking to understand how the conscious mind works. Over time this will become more quantifiable. Ultimately, it will be removed from the realm of philosophy and placed within the bounds of a specific science. Yet that won't change the fact that everything you know which is not innate, is derived either from your own first hand sensory experiences, or by being told that it is so. If it is derived through your sensory experiences, it is colored by your perception of what you sense; and if it is derived through instruction, it is a description which you do not know first-hand, but rather one which you must trust.

So we still ask ourselves what we genuinely know. We still ponder if we can distinguish between reality, and the appearance of reality. Perhaps reality in the universe is akin to the view of a painting as seen through the eyes of a painter who paints the individual brush strokes and shades in a painting, but our view of the universe is like the view of the painter's patrons who see only a face in a portrait; the appearance of reality to us differs from the painter's reality.

We still think of mathematical ideas as something called thought, and the colors we see as something called perception, yet we do not know where abstract thought ends and where the senses take over, or even if the distinction we make between thoughts and senses is a proper way of classifying our experiences. How does a non-physical thought affect the physical? Why does a placebo ever have an effect?

Philosophers still ask if the foundation of all things is spiritual in nature—a view that returns us to Plato and his idea world—or if everything is ultimately derived from concrete material substances—a view that returns us to Aristotle.

They continue to debate the question of what is changeable in the universe and what cannot be changed, and whether there is a fixed right and wrong.

Are mind and body separate? Is each person

really two, spirit (a separate soul) and matter? Or is each of us one whole? Is Plato right or is Aristotle right?

Perhaps the declared division between mind and matter is just an attempt to organize a deep mystery so that it can be accessible to people. Perhaps the difficulty of explaining human consciousness and self-awareness is the reason that some divide mind and body in the first place, and theorize that a separate soul exists. Once the existence of a separate soul is believed, some will search for immortality and for salvation from death; and some will search to find rebirth. Others use separation to argue that people are sinners, and in need of salvation. Sin is said by some to be an estrangement from God. Salvation, sometimes called redemption, is said to be the deliverance.

Is each of us born a sinner in need of salvation or might we have been born worthwhile?

How are humans connected to the whole of the universe? Are we the center of everything as some say, or are we a part on the periphery? Maybe in some way beyond our understanding and beyond the limitations implicit in our questions, we can be both simultaneously.

And philosophy goes round and round, yet through this maze I hope you can begin to trace the origins of some beliefs (including conceptions of God), which have been imparted to you.

While you do so, recognize an evolution. An evolution of religion; an evolution from thoughts of God as the cause of victory and defeat, to a giver of human freewill and self-responsibility; an evolution of identity from one in which personal identity was secondary to the collective group, to one in which individual conscience, self-responsibility and personal autonomy are paramount; an evolution of human morality from concerns about the outward results of a person's actions, to a morality which focuses on a person's intent. These evolutions coincide with the ability to control nature and the ability to understand the sciences. Even so, many of the same questions remain.

Is a deity infinite and present in all things? Or is the Creator external to his creation? Are there insurmountable barriers to God? What is of the nature of God? As the sciences expand, symbolic interpretations of ancient texts replace literal ones; less and less is directly ascribed to God and more and more is indirectly ascribed to God. For instance, the rainbow was once viewed as the sign of a covenant given by God directly to Noah (and to all else that came out of the ark) to mark the fact that there would never be another flood to destroy earth. As we learned about the cause of rainbows (a refractive dispersion of sunlight in drops of rain), the tie between God and rainbows has grown more distant.

Still we ask: Where does everything come from? (Can this truly be answered if we don't yet have a satisfactory understanding of the nature of matter?) What is the meaning in life? What governs our behavior?

We all wish to find reason for our conclusions, yet our answers to deeply spiritual questions must derive from faith. A tension exists between our ability to reason and faith. Answers which conform to our reason are bounded by universal laws within space and time which are necessary for a physical being to exist. But our imagination tells us that the universe which can be experienced or verified by humans, as physical beings, may be only one aspect of the whole of the universe.

So how can you be certain that you truly know what you think you know? If you reflect on it, you can't be absolutely certain.

Yet by examining differing answers to great questions, your mind expands—and this will help you to find answers which have meaning to you.

The Books

Answers offered by the ancient writings of all major religions have had a great influence on the common threads of spiritual thinking.

In the West, three books—the Jewish Torah, the Christian New Testament and the Islamic Koran—have been the most prevalent.

There is a great deal of good that humanity has learned from all three Books. They all contain codes of moral behavior; codes that in some measure did not exist before these Books came to be; codes that most of us take for granted today. I believe these texts were written to be in plain language—plain, that is, for the elite of the day who could read. Starting with the Torah, the greatness in the Books is the decree that society is to operate on the basis of law—a basis beyond the whim of any individual. All three Books have propelled civilization forward.

All three Books also served, and continue to serve, as community guides to help people find an understanding of God, the universe, and life; and to help people manage their everyday world.

But are they, individually or collectively, the final word regarding humanity?

Humanity continuously learns about itself and the universe. It is inevitable that history will show the conclusions of each generation to be faulty in some respect. Though all three Books offer great lessons from which we can learn, they also contain contradictions, inaccuracies, and lessons of morality which do not stand the test of time.

For example, in the Torah, God is repeatedly said to have given orders to kill people for reasons which we would consider unacceptable today. The Torah claims that God sent serpents to kill people who complained about being forced to leave Egypt and complained about the quality of the food on the journey (Numbers 21:4-6). The Torah also claims that God stated that if a town far away accepts the Israelites' terms of peace, all the townspeople will serve the Israelites as forced labor. But if the townspeople do not surrender, all the men are to be killed, and everything else, including the women, can be taken as bounty (Deuteronomy 20:10-14).

In the New Testament, Jesus is generally portrayed lovingly. But Jesus is still occasionally portrayed as mean-spirited, at least from today's point of view. For example, Jesus is said to have made a fig tree wither because the tree did not have fruit to feed him when he was hungry (Matthew 21:18-19).

And in the Koran, in the name of God, men are allowed to have sex with their women slaves (Sura 23:5-6). Obviously, even the idea of women slaves, let alone the approval of sex in this context, is morally unacceptable today.

The fact that one generation speculates wrongly about any matter is of no consequence unless it condemns future generations to live by its erroneous speculations.

Question closely the beliefs of people who lived centuries ago because those beliefs may not lead you toward meaning and inner peace.

Socrates would have been delighted to learn of Isaac Newton's Law of Universal Gravitation, and would have modified his view of solar and planetary movement accordingly. Newton would have been thrilled to learn of Albert Einstein's theory of relativity, and modified his views accordingly.

Be open to explanations about humanity and the universe which intuitively make more sense to you than those offered in the Torah, the New Testament and the Koran. It makes little sense to think that the authors of the Books, or the God described in those books, would condemn or ridicule humanity for striding forward.

If your reason or intuition guides you to accept humanity's growth, do not ignore it. It stands to reason that the reflections of God contained in the Books would differ if your ancestors possessed the knowledge available to you.

Challenging the Answers of Others

Through the answers imparted to you by your parents, other loved ones, friends and acquaintances, you are influenced by many sources. By challenging the answers of others, your mind expands.

Though in the broadest philosophical context it may be fair to say that, like Socrates, we each know nothing, within the framework of scientific assumptions, we know a great deal upon which we base, or can base, our beliefs.

Some things which ring false at first, are ultimately adopted as true. For most of history people assumed that the earth was flat. Without the aid of empirical scientific evidence, the fact that the earth is a spherical globe from which we do not fall off would seem untrue.

When Copernicus shared his knowledge that

the sun did not revolve around the earth, but rather, it was the earth which revolves around the sun, he did so at great personal peril. In the 16th century, the false certainty that the earth was the center of the universe was essential to many religious believers.

Although a false belief can bring inner peace, no one alive today would choose to go backwards and readopt the false 16th century belief.

Consider a lesson which can be learned from the story of Copernicus: Humanity will ultimately choose to know more, even if that knowledge challenges convention and is uncomfortable.

The diminishing of ignorance benefits humanity and propels civilization forward. By sharing knowledge each generation can stand on the shoulders of the generation before, and each person is supported by humanity's collective knowledge.

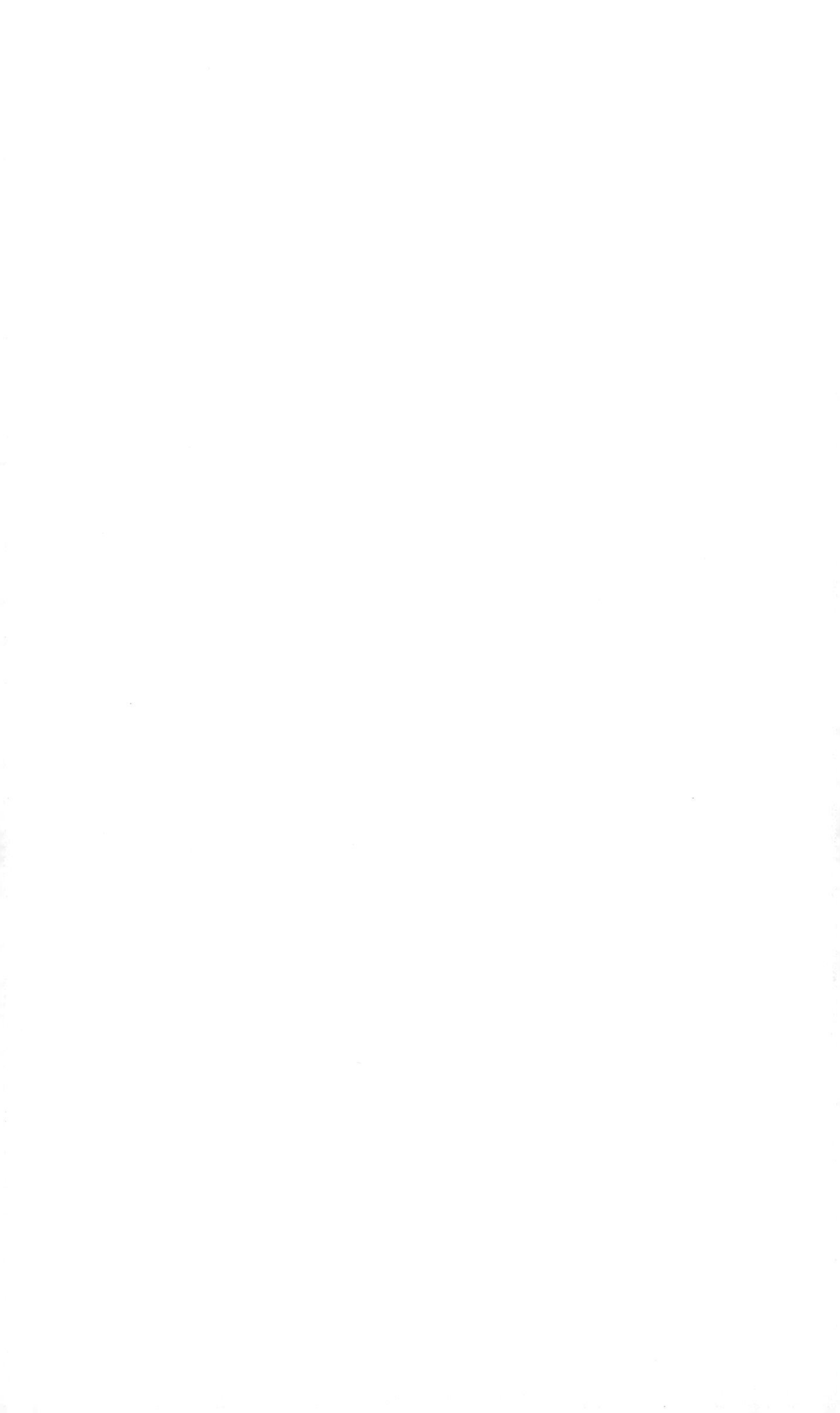

PART II

Toward Meaning and Peace

Harmonizing Beliefs and Actions

All beliefs require faith, and faith requires you to make assumptions of one sort or another.

The first part of this book was meant to challenge you to uncover and question your assumptions. The second part of this book is meant, in part, to reinforce two ideas which are probably evident to you: one, if the actions you take in life do not reflect your true beliefs, you will experience an inner conflict which does not lend itself toward experiencing peace; and two, a negative belief (such as thinking that the nature of humankind is evil) precludes your peace, even if your actions do reflect that belief.

It is not easy to change a negative belief. It is hard to imagine that a new belief can be adopted merely through affirmation, or longing. Yet, a reflective change in an underlying assumption is likely to cause a true change in belief, and so, a change in everything about you which flows from that belief.

The second part of the book is also meant to offer you, or to reinforce in you, beliefs which I believe greatly enhance the ability most people already have to experience meaning and inner peace—the seeds of a life lived in harmony with yourself and others.

These beliefs are not new. Through the generations, all of them have been offered at one time or another, but their truth cannot be proved.

You may accept some of these beliefs intuitively, yet for one reason or another, you may not have succeeded in guiding your actions by them. One cause for this lack of success may be that no one has given you persuasive reasons why placing your faith in, *and* guiding your actions by these beliefs, enhances meaning and inner peace. In the pages which follow, I have tried to do so.

Of equal importance, the beliefs I offer may be ones which you have not adopted because they do not flow from your current assumptions. Consider them only if, upon reflection, they make sense to you and touch you at your core.

God ~

No one can impose their spiritual description of God on you because no one is literally able to describe God.

◆

I believe a force beyond our understanding of the universe exists.

Some have given a name to this force. Others do not. Some do not believe that such a force exists. Yet many who say they do not believe, really mean that they do not believe in a particular description that is used by others.

Descriptions of god(s) have changed through time and varied by culture, yet the differing stories told have served a common purpose; to touch us deeply, to spark a visceral and spiritual connection to something greater than ourselves.

Eastern stories speak of gods as manifestations of an energy that at its source is impersonal and unknown to us.

Western stories speak of one personal deity as

the original cause of creation. This unknown is named Yahweh, Jehovah, Allah, God.

Some view God as a metaphor for the mystery beyond anything we can classify—the mystery of existence and our being.

No matter what the view, around the world, people share the search for understanding; trying to connect with that which they cannot see, hear, or touch.

God is showered with descriptions and attributes; God is talked about through metaphors and analogies. We do this in an attempt to transcend beyond our human shell. We do this in an attempt to bring God into the world we understand.

But do not confuse descriptions of the unknown with understanding the unknown. Do not confuse an ability to name the unknown—the name God—with knowing the unknown.

Human experience takes place within space and in the course of time. But if God's relationship to the universe is not tied to our human conception of time, and God transcends our world of matter, energy, space and time, God cannot be described literally. Words are simply not adequate to the task.

Alternatively, if God is the sum of all that is, this

too defies our descriptions. We humans do not know all that is.

Ultimately then, each description we have of God is limited by the scope of what the human mind can experience, and each description is limited by our reason, senses, and imagination.

Yet thousands of attributes have been used throughout time to describe God or attempt to capture God's essence. Some ascribe omnipotence to God. Others ascribe historical deeds, physical abilities, or emotional qualities to God. Still others ascribe powers of miracle to God.

Any description of God which you adopt as your own acts to shape your view of life and the universe. These descriptions can be a source of strength and enlightenment, or they can be a source of conflict and inner turmoil. As each of us matures, we search for an understanding that touches us more deeply, yet we may be burdened with the concrete descriptions we were able to understand in our youth. A young mind is not fully developed; it is only capable of understanding simple descriptions of God.

Examine your own beliefs about God to see if they touch you or if they are negative for you. Do you believe that God makes demands on you? Do you believe that God punishes you, makes your choices for you, controls your destiny without your say, cares about your sexuality, or decides whether or not you get into heaven? Do your beliefs bring you closer to God, or do they separate you and stunt your ability to experience peace?

Descriptions of God that are ingrained in your subconscious, may not spiritually ring true for you. Descriptions that touched people living thousands of years ago may not be useful to you, just as descriptions which touch you may not be useful to someone born tomorrow.

God can have no comparison. Yet speaking of God requires comparison. And because comparisons are made, descriptions take hold in consciousness. Once a description is ingrained, the quest to connect with God invariably centers on asking questions about God based on the assumed truth of that particular description. But your faith is not made less pure by embracing God as other than male, tall, or bearded. If a particular description does not touch you deeply and intuitively, let it go. If a description does not ring true for you, and you don't discard it, your questions will misguide you. A question which has a false premise is nonsensical and cannot be answered. The question must be changed in order to arrive at an answer which is meaningful or enlightening for you.

Consider the question which was probably asked by sailors of yesteryear: What happens to us if our ship goes over the edge of the earth?

No matter how carefully they considered this question, the differing catastrophic answers of all the sailors have proved to be equally incorrect. This is because their question falsely *assumes* that if they sailed far enough from the center of the earth, their ship would indeed fall off. Today we know that no answer to this question can be meaningful.

Some people ask: How could an all-powerful and all-good God allow evil to rise to power and cause the indescribable human suffering of the Jewish, Armenian and Cambodian Holocausts? But the question assumes a particular description of God's being to be a true manifestation of God. It forces a conclusion that God is either not all powerful, not all good, "works in mysterious ways," or does not exist at all.

If God is not limited by the boundaries of dimensions and time, no question which measures God on a humanly-defined linear scale of more or less power, or more or less goodness, can have a meaningful answer.

Is the universe a phenomenon of God, which is separate and apart from God, or is the universe an indivisible part of God? We cannot know whether God is external to his creation, or a part of it. Perhaps the answer is both, but perhaps the question is faulty.

Clear your mind of all notions about God. Think of the awe and wonder of that which we have named God, yet unencumbered by attributes or descriptions. With this openness, you may be more able to understand and appreciate other people's descriptions of God, their way of bringing themselves closer to—and connecting with—God.

Your exploration does not require you to describe God in a particular way.

God need not be thought of as merciful or unmerciful, just or unjust, or as a supreme being who rewards or punishes people for doing right or wrong.

God need not be thought of as angry or jealous, as all-knowing, or as having either more or less capabilities or limitations.

God need not be thought of as a being who can

only be accessed through intermediaries, or through adherence to particularly defined rules.

Peoples all over the world profess to believe in God, yet debate each other regarding particular manifestations of God. These manifestations must be of no consequence if no one is literally able to describe God. Do not let the descriptions of God which are offered by the religion of your birth become a barrier to your personal spiritual experience if those descriptions do not speak to you.

In your quest to spiritually connect with God, listen to yourself from within. Allow your personal faith to guide you.

The Universe and Scientific Discovery

Science enhances our spiritual quest.

It is not a threat to it.

◆

Science enhances our spiritual quest by giving us more information. But science cannot tell us *why* the universe exists, or where the substance which comprises it comes from.

Science helps us understand the workings of the universe, useful information in answering mechanical questions. Scientific explanations of creation and evolution can be accepted or discarded through reason. Contradictory explanations can be accepted or discarded based on evidence. But Einstein, Newton and Galileo could not provide the answers to our deeper questions.

So where does the universe come from? Cosmologists believe that matter and energy are interchangeable and that about 15 billion years ago, all matter in the universe came forth from a point in which every place and every time was identical. It exploded. This is referred to as the Big Bang. Out of pure energy came the potent particle which is the spark of the genesis that followed. Everything that exists is part of this genesis particle. As the universe expanded and cooled, darkness was everywhere. Light formed anew with the formation of the first stars.

There is a great deal of geological evidence which leads to the belief that the earth was formed over four and one half billion years ago, when our solar system came to be.

As a result of the Big Bang, cosmologists say that roughly one hundred billion galaxies exist in the universe, and each of these galaxies consists, on average, of about one hundred billion stars. They have identified galaxies which are more than ten billion light years away form earth. In our galaxy, the Milky Way, about 400 billion stars are said to exist. One of these stars is our sun.

Each time the earth, the third planet from the sun, completes one elliptical orbit around the sun, we experience it as a year. Each time the earth makes a revolution, we experience it as day and night.

A light year is defined as the distance light

travels in one year. The Milky Way itself is said to be 90,000 light-years wide, but our sun is only eight light minutes away from the earth. As we view the sun, we see it as it was eight minutes ago. Indeed all light which we see from a star reveals how the star existed when the light emanated. It does not reveal how the star exists today. This is why it is said that when we view the stars we are looking into the past. The further away a star is from us, the further into the past we look. The distance to the nearest star from our sun is four light years. Thus, we see it as it was four years ago.

The nearest galaxy to our own Milky Way is the Andromeda nebula. It is located two million light years away from earth. We see it as it was two million years ago.

There is a great deal of scientific evidence which suggests that all galaxies are moving away from each other, and that the actual distance between galaxies is increasing all the time.

Will the universe continue to expand as a result of inertia? Will it reach perfect balance and stop? Or will it go through cycles of expansion and contraction, or collapse on itself as a result of gravity, and start anew with another big bang? Perhaps none of these are so.

Perhaps humanity's ultimate purpose is to make sure that the universe lives forever. Perhaps the universe both began and always existed in a manner beyond our comprehension.

Our human ability to perceive may limit us to a partial understanding of the universe because, in our experience, for something to physically exist, it must be comprised of three dimensions and exist in time. Indeed, the universe, as some define it, may be only a part of a bigger picture.

As we discover more, a new theory may be put forth which better-explains the workings of the universe. The Big Bang theory is supported by a great deal of evidence, but it is only a theory, not a fact.

Today, physicists are still struggling to marry the concepts of quantum mechanics, which seems to govern the subatomic world, and general relativity, which seems to govern the workings of the universe from the moment after the Big Bang occurred. This is the search for one unified theory of everything.

Yet even a unified theory will be unlikely to reveal to us whether existence requires creation or a creator, or whether something preceded a so-called creator; for this, we must have faith, or not have faith.

Often people who fight science do so in order to preserve their particular description of God. If you are not threatened by science, scientific discovery may allow you to grow as humanity learns more. Through discovery, science can open the doors to experiencing ever greater levels of awe and wonder.

Evolution on Earth

God and evolution are not in conflict.

◆

There is a great deal of biological evidence which leads to the belief in the theory of evolution.

The evidence suggests that life on earth began three to four billion years ago, and that all living organisms which exist on earth today, whether classified as plants or animals, are based on the element carbon. Without carbon, there would be no life on earth.

The molecule we call DNA is the common ingredient within carbon-based organisms which separates all that we consider *living* from all that we regard as *non-living* matter. It is the hereditary structure found in all living cells, not just humanity, and governs the ability of each cell to divide itself into two identical cells.

The evidence of evolution on earth is based, in large measure, on the fossil remains found in stratified layers of rock, and on the differences which can be seen within a living species in its various habitats. It can be understood as follows: There is a continuous variation of individuals within the same species, and there are too many of each species born to survive. Thus, only the strong can survive; the strong being the individual species members which best adapt to survive in a particular environment. This is what Charles Darwin referred to as nature's natural selection.

Though strong scientific evidence exists that supports this theory of evolution and no scientific evidence exists which disproves it, as with other theories, it is a theory, it is not a fact. Neither Darwin nor anyone else familiar with scientific processes would suggest otherwise.

For a true appreciation of how long scientists believe humans have existed in relationship to the age of the universe, Carl Sagan compressed the time span of what is theorized to be a 15-billion-year-old universe, into a span of one year. By doing so, Sagan described the Big Bang as having occurred on the dawning of the year, January 1; the origin of the Milky Way galaxy occurred on May 1; our solar system was formed on September 9; the earth was formed on September 14; the origin of life on earth began about September 25; the first humans appeared on December 31, at about 10:30 p.m.! On December 31 at 11:59:20 p.m., agriculture was invented; Jesus was born at 11:59:56 p.m.; the Renaissance in Europe occurred 3 seconds later at 11:59:59 p.m.

All of humanity's recorded history occurs in the final ten seconds of the last day of the year. Today, we are in the first second of the new year!

Does this picture of evolution make humanity less special than the picture painted by the Bible—the picture in which humanity is specially created on the sixth day of creation in God's own image? Surely not. It is amazing that in the universe, humanity exists. Perhaps in your mind, as in mine, the likelihood of evolution makes the force beyond our understanding of the universe more amazing.

Humanity ~

Self-awareness is a special gift.

◆

There seems to be an ordered imbalance to the universe which produces differences in form. It is theorized that in the past, particles and atoms began building themselves into different molecules, and molecules began building themselves into life. Life led to self-awareness, and self-awareness led to the desire to be enlightened; to ask questions about all which is existence.

A being must be aware of its own thinking to be able to ask about the universe and its own existence; it is the precondition to seeking understanding. It is a gift each of us shares. It is a gift to be respected in others.

The Universal Connection ⌣

We each share a common bond with the universe and with everything that exists in it.

◆

For all its vastness and seeming diversity, many scientists believe that everything that appears to us to exist in the universe, may be made of different combinations of the same elementary building block.

If this is so, trillions of these identical building blocks combine in such a way as to create extremely complex living organisms; and yet, presumably an individual building block need not be part of any combination at all.

Everything viewed from a human perspective as being of greater or lesser worth, is made of the elementary building block.

We, and everything around us, whether energy or matter, are made of this block. It combines to create the earth, the stars and space; it combines to create flowers, trees, and animals; it combines to create iron, steel and a spec of dust. Think of it as the ingredient that binds the cosmos, or perhaps, the ingredient that binds us to God.

Perhaps each building block was present in one form or another before you or I were born, and will be present long after you and I die. Perhaps each building block may even be eternal, that is, present as long as a universe exists.

Look into the night sky and free your mind to experience the universe from this different perspective. Try to sense your oneness with everything that surrounds you. When you do, you are less likely to sense ill will toward anyone or anything. You are more likely to sense peace with all that exists in the universe.

Free Will and Destiny ~

How you live and act as a human being is your choice to make. Believe in your own free will.

◆

At the time when some ancient Greeks began seeking natural, rather than supernatural explanations of events, their countrymen were still journeying to oracles to ask about their fate. Many people would not take an important action in life without such a consultation. At one of these shrines, known as the Oracle at Delphi, the travelers posed their questions to the priests of the Oracle who, in turn, passed the questions on to a woman chosen to serve as a priestess. The priestess entered into a trance by eating laurel leafs and inhaling vapors from a chasm in the ground. Once the priestess was in a trance, the questioners believed the Oracle's god, Apollo, spoke through her. The answers of the priestess were cryptic, and so, the attending priests and others functionaries interpreted them. But even if Apollo actually knew a person's fate *and* spoke through the priestess, the questioner was still relying on a fallible human's interpretations of Apollo's proclamations.

Pierre-Simon Laplace, the French mathematician who lived from 1749 to 1827, theorized that if an intelligence, at any given moment, knew the laws of nature *and* the exact position of all matter in the universe, *and* had the capacity to analyze the data and condense it into a single formula, nothing would ever be unknown to it because it could calculate everything from this information. The intelligence would know when life would form, and when humans would become self-aware. It would also know what you will be doing two minutes from now because it would know how each neuron in your brain will fire, and the effect this will cause.

If Laplace's picture of the universe is true, everything that happens is predetermined. This view appears to preclude free will. Each of us would be no different than a computer formulated to handle a computation. When a computer is programmed, the designer knows the computer's steps before the computer performs them—only the computer itself is in the dark.

A similar view is shared by present-day thinkers called Determinists who believe that in an ordered universe all events in nature are caused. They believe that all that will occur has already been set in motion from the time of the distant past, whether or not an all-knowing intelligence exists.

But what if the operation of the universe defies definitive calculation? The theory of quantum mechanics holds that both the precise position of a subatomic particle and its momentum cannot be simultaneously known to an observer in our universe. And what if the universe contains infinite complexity in a finite space? This is contemplated in the mathematical principles of fractal geometry. Quantum mechanics and fractal geometry seem to insert an element of unpredictability into an orderly mathematical world—an unpredictability that may defeat the idea that all is predetermined.

Perhaps God chose to create a universe which contains free will and sin, and good and evil, rather than creating a universe devoid of choice. Without free will there can be no sin because the absence of free will precludes actually *choosing* sin. If sin is not freely chosen, it cannot be truly sin. Likewise, without good there can be no evil because if evil is not chosen, but rather is predetermined, it cannot be truly called evil.

The debate over which reality governs human action has been going on for thousands of years. In essence, proponents of destiny (determinists and fatalists) believe that whatever is, was to be. Proponents of free will believe that we have the liberty to act in ways other than the way we eventually choose.

Yet, must life be viewed as either being of free will or of destiny? What of our own limitations of understanding the universe? Einstein said we can never go faster than the speed of light because time slows as it approaches the speed of light. His theory of relativity—which rejects the idea of absolute time—helped to explain previously-inexplicable phenomena in the universe. But is the explanation correct? Or are the seemingly accurate predictions of this theory only a function of the limitations of our mind?

If the laws which we believe govern the universe are in reality only laws which are a product of the human mind, limited by our perspective of time, then perhaps it is not necessary for time itself to go forward, or for that matter backwards. If there is an existence outside the scope of space and time, all that we think we know may exist in a manner which is beyond our ability to conceive. Therefore, we cannot definitively dismiss the possibility of parallel universes or an individual's multiple and simultaneous existences.

We do not know what exists outside the boundaries of space and time. As it is not the nature of a tree to walk, it is not in our nature to be outside the boundaries of space and time. We do not know with finality whether destiny or free will rule human life, or whether a combination of the two governs human life. Some believe that free will and determinism are compatible and that the debate is merely a semantic one. They dismiss fatalism as superstition.

From a human perspective, we guide our conscious lives as if we have free will, whether or not this is an illusion. The belief in a God who knows everything is not necessarily incompatible with free will. Just as your awareness of what happened yesterday does not make that knowledge the *cause* of what happened, foreknowledge does not make the future happen. Even if God knows an outcome, it does not mean that your will is destroyed.

Whether or not events are cosmically set, we do not know in advance which choices will confront us and which decisions we will make. As rational beings we have to deliberate and apply reason to the question of what to do. If we knew that determinism was true, our decision-making process would still be relevant. It seems to fill the gap between our desires and what we actually choose to do.

By believing in your own free will, in essence, you acknowledge that you are responsible for your choices and your actions. The benefit of acknowledging this responsibility is an appreciation that you can impact the direction of your future.

Inner Well-Being ~

You alone are responsible for your inner well-being; no one else can be.

◆

Many people do not feel inner peace because they have stopped listening to themselves, and instead look to their peers to validate what they should do, how they should behave, and what values they should hold dear. Harmonizing your actions with someone else's beliefs does not lead to inner peace. Your actions must reflect *your* true beliefs.

Listen to your inner-self. Others can teach you wisdom in life, but some can lead you astray as well. If you are to achieve peace, it must be done from within. Ultimately, only you can know how to be true to yourself, what is right for you, and what makes you happy.

Many people seek to blame someone else when something goes wrong in their life. This gnaws at them and stops them from feeling peace.

Certainly others do things which can make you either happy or miserable, but others cannot determine how you will feel about what they say or do, or how you will react to what they say or do.

Things, which some consider unfair, happen in life; things which can change your material well-being, your standing in the community, and your heath.

Yet, how you feel about what is happening is not the result of what is actually happening, but rather, is the result of your interpretation of what is happening. You alone determine how you experience life's circumstances. You alone determine your responses.

This is not to say that you can turn your feelings on and off like a light switch. We are, after all, emotional beings, and the experience of your life would not be a human experience if you did not feel the gamut of emotions from sadness to anger to joy.

Though it seems harder to take responsibility for your inner well-being than to blame others for any pain you feel, blaming others can only bring momentary relief, it cannot bring you peace.

By taking responsibility for your inner well-being, you increase your ability to feel benevolence, kindness, and compassion toward others because you allow no outside force to be held responsible for any lack of well-being. This is the road to true inner peace. And as inner peace can be momentary or long lasting, the more responsibility you accept for your own inner well-being, the more inner peace you will likely experience.

Principles ⌣

Treating others as you wish others to treat you, really does lead to peace.

◆

Rabbi Hillel said: "What is hateful to you, do not do unto your neighbor. This is the entire Torah; all the rest is commentary."

Jesus said: "So whatever you wish that men would do to you, do so to them; for this is the law and the prophets."

Buddha said: "For the sake of the welfare of others, however great, let no one neglect their own welfare."

But why do they say these things? As with all beliefs, it cannot be proved that living life by these principles is right. Yet it is evident that these principles are not merely the creation of cultural biases. They are ageless and transcend all human cultures because they recognize something fundamental in our being: **each of us wishes to be treated well.** This is why it seems difficult to feel peace when you feel ill will toward someone, or treat someone poorly. But it is easy to feel peace after treating someone kindly. When you know how you wish others to treat you, you know the way to treat yourself. But, how do you go about treating others well?

Treating others the way you wish to be treated is not as simple as projecting what you think your needs would be if you were in their situation. People have differing views of what it means to be treated well. In some instances, this difference exists because another person's underlying assumptions about unprovable matters are different than yours. Other times, perspectives differ merely because each of us looks at situations through the filtered color of our unique life experiences.

Allowing room for others to see, hear and feel things differently increases your ability to treat them as they wish to be treated. Each attempt you make to be aware of, and empathize with, what someone else is thinking or feeling will make it easier for you to understand and accept their behavior. It also increases your ability to be at peace should you feel that they have not treated you well. In addition, it reduces your inclination to pre-judge others harshly.

Think of how unfair it is to quickly pass judgement on someone else. Even great empathy does not allow you to actually see other people's thoughts and feelings. Their thoughts and feelings are invisible to you, yet they are likely to be as complex as your own.

In the end, we each judge ourself by our intentions. Because we cannot see other people's intentions, we tend to judge others by their actions, that is, by our perception of their actions. If your actions (as perceived by others) do not reflect your intentions, others will have a different view of you than you would wish. If the actions of others (as perceived by you) do not mirror their intent, you will have a different view of them than they would wish. Be mindful that this constantly causes misunderstandings which prevent peace.

Some argue that treating others well in order to gain inner peace is nothing more than an act of selfishness. But their argument rests on defining *anything* a person does which makes them feel good, regardless of motive, as selfish. This is nothing but a semantical argument. It would be like calling the color we call red by the name blue. Even if everyone agrees to do so, it would not change the actual color, it would only change the name.

Inner peace is unlike any other desire in life. Attaining joy from your actions, and having them lead to inner peace, does not make a person selfish. Being selfish is having no regard for the well-being of others.

One is selfish when acting only for him or herself. Treating others and yourself well centers on everyone's well-being. It really does lead to peace.

Moral Values ⌣

Human morality is not relative.

◆

Allowing room for others to see, hear and feel things differently does not mean abandoning moral judgment.

We do not know with certainty whether moral values exist independently of humanity or whether morality is a conception of the human mind. But no matter the source, the words we use to describe moral values, words such as truth, equality, liberty, loyalty, justice and mercy, express conflicting ideas of what humanity holds to be right and good.

A moral dilemma seems to be a consequence which exists when we are unsure of how to treat each other. The words listed above are used in an attempt to capture our thoughts about how we wish to be treated.

But those words do not eliminate the conflict, they only serve to illuminate it for discussion and growth. Consider our ideals of justice and mercy. Isn't mercy offered when justice seems to be too harsh and unkind to be right and good?

There doesn't appear to be one answer to moral dilemmas which can be proven right for all people and for all time. Consider the search of the moral philosophers who reflect upon the common experience of humanity.

Many begin their search for definitive answers about right and wrong with the assumption that there is an absolute truth which can be found. But if deductive reasoning begins only after the making of such an assumption, it cannot lead to indisputable proof.

This is why the arguments of philosophers from Aristotle to Sartre fail to be intuitively right for everyone.

Yet even though moral dilemmas exist, right and wrong are not arbitrary. Everyone's individual values are not morally equivalent because not all assumptions which affect a person's beliefs are of equal moral force. An assumption which ignores the fact that every person wishes to be treated well is immoral **from humanity's viewpoint**. When a person's behavior cannot be reconciled with an underlying intent to treat others well, that behavior cannot be condoned as morally acceptable.

Thus, on most general matters involving questions of right and wrong, there is agreement among people—even those who choose to do wrong. The beliefs that one should not commit murder, lie or steal can be derived from the principle of treating other people as you wish them to treat you, no matter what the source of the principle. Since no one wants these acts done to them, it is understood that it is wrong to do them to others.

When a moral dilemma presents itself to you, if the choice you make reflects the principles of treating others and yourself the way you wish to be treated, it is a good choice, the right one for you. It is a choice in which you can find peace.

Right and Wrong ~

The more often you do what you know in your heart is right, the more peace you will feel.

◆

People who do wrong sometimes prosper in life. Accept this, but do not confuse material well-being with inner well-being. Do not confuse self-indulgence with being true to one's self. Those who treat others poorly will almost inevitably live a life of fear and suspicion, regardless of material prosperity. For them, inner peace and contentment is unlikely because a belief system which leads to a disregard of others will inescapably produce inner loneliness, and not inner peace.

When you are uncertain of what is right and wrong, consider the answers to these six questions. Your answers will assist you in identifying right from wrong. They will assist you in harmonizing your actions with your beliefs.

1) Would you be proud of yourself for doing what you are contemplating? Make sure that what you are doing feels right to you.

2) Would it be alright with you if your friends and family learned that you actually did what you are contemplating? The decisions you make, but which you hope no one will discover, are usually wrong decisions.

3) Does what you are about to do seem fair to you? Consider the consequences of your actions on other beings and the environment.

4) How would you advise another if the choice was his or hers to make? Consider the soundness of taking your own advice.

5) If the person you admire most was confronted with the same situation, how would he or she handle it? The manner in which you think he or she would handle a problem is probably the manner in which you believe you should handle it.

6) Are you doing what is right because you expect a special reward beyond your joy in doing it? Inner peace is found when motives are pure. Expect no reward, earthly or other.

Choose wisely. Use your ability to reason. Use your heart. Make decisions which harmonize your actions with your beliefs and you will be at peace.

Religion ⌣

No religion has a monopoly on truth.

◆

All religions are guides to help people find an understanding of God, the universe, and life; and all religions are guides to help people manage the everyday world.

Faith in the truth of a particular religion can lead to meaning and inner peace. But any religion will produce misery on earth if its adherents come to think of it, and the story of life it tells, as the sole provider of absolute and literal truth. This is because the conviction that their religion is literally true condemns, in their eyes, all other religions to being literally false. It leads adherents of that religion to think of themselves as closer to God and in other ways superior to adherents of other religions.

This thinking has led zealous believers throughout time to pity, hate and even kill non-believers.

This continuing human tragedy is not likely of God.

After all, the leading predictor of a person's religion is their environment. Most Catholics have Catholic parents. Most Hindus have Hindu parents. Most Jews have Jewish parents. And most Muslims have Muslim parents. Mix the children at birth and most children would grow up comfortably in the faith of their environmental parents, not their biological ones. Each of these religions is imparted, none is innate.

Yet so many adhere to their religion as literal truth. And they consider conforming to the strict letter of their religious law as an extra burden. Discipline can be rewarding, but nothing is easier than not thinking. And nothing requires as little thinking as adhering to set, definitive rules, no matter what they are.

It is not likely that you possess an ability to reason just so that a force beyond our understanding of the universe could ask you to ignore it.

By accepting the religion of your choice as a guide to help you become enlightened, rather than a literal truth, you allow yourself to break down the barrier between people; you allow others to have alternative guides in their quest to find answers. You allow yourself a better opportunity to live in harmony with others.

Death

There is no reason to fear death.

◆

As a beginning implies an end, birth implies death. It is a part of life.

What happens when people die? Maybe something, maybe nothing. Religions talk of death through the stories of the departed's journey to another time, another place, or another plane. Yet are the dead reborn to live future lives? Or are only the dead who are deserving allowed to live eternally in heavenly peace? No one is able to know for certain.

But no matter what you believe happens after death, it is hard to maintain that your particular belief ought to alter how you live and act in this life.

If, for example, you were certain that nothing happened after death, would it make selfishness more joyous or inner peace less desirable? Would you be likely to achieve peace if you treated others poorly and thought only of yourself?

Of course, if you were certain that Heaven and Hell existed, you would undoubtedly alter any behavior you thought was poor. But if the only reason you altered your behavior was to obtain a non-earthly reward after death (or feared punishment for poor behavior) your motive would not be pure. It would be merely pragmatic. If Heaven's keeper took motive into account, you would not be admitted.

It is said that living a lifetime in harmony with yourself and others leads to fewer regrets, and to knowing less sorrow from death. If you accept that your belief about what happens after death ought not cause you to alter your behavior in this life, it is pointless to fear death. It will come when it comes. What will happen will happen.

Time ⌣

You determine how you allocate your time; no one else does.

◆

You decide what is worthwhile and what is not. Your choices can be difficult.

How does anyone choose between unconditional love of all, and prioritized love among a few? Should a person spend time being involved in the community at the expense of spending time with a spouse or child? Must a doctor work every night if there are people in need, or can he or she have some time for other pursuits?

People will reach different conclusions, and only you can determine what is right for you. These choices are not between right and wrong, or good and bad, and the answers are not apparent.

Your life is lived within the limitations of a 24-hour day, and in a lifetime consisting of 24-hour days you cannot do all things.

Often, people give time to whomever or whatever makes the loudest demand. But if you let an outside force dictate your choices, you are likely to find that you will not be at peace with what you are doing.

Set aside time to reflect upon achieving harmony between your beliefs and your actions. Be aware of decisions regarding your time that are being made for you. By using your beliefs to guide you, you can consciously decide how to best allocate your own time.

There is much that you can learn from your past experiences but many people spend time *dwelling* on their past, and what might have been. This self-inflicted torment ruins their present and their future. It is impossible to change the past. It is, however, possible to spend your time in a manner which lets you take control of the present and future.

It is said that people near the end of life have regrets about what they did not attempt to do, or make time to do, but few have regrets for failing to succeed when they had given a thing their time, and their best effort. This is why failure should not be feared. Rather, it seems that you are more likely to find inner peace when you give time to attempt to do that which is important to you.

Epilogue ⌣

Consider these beliefs. Adopt them as your own only if they make sense to you and touch you at your core. They may guide you toward meaning in life, and help you to find inner peace:

1) The act of naming God is not the same as understanding God. By naming an unknown, all you have done is name it.

2) You alone are responsible for your inner well-being.

3) Two good people, given the exact same circumstance, can come to different conclusions regarding what is right to do.

4) Giving others room to find their own way and taking room to find yours enhances peace.

5) When you judge another, it is only a judgment of how you perceive that person, not necessarily a judgment of who he or she really is.

6) Treating others the way you wish to be treated necessitates that you practice privately what you advocate publicly. It necessitates that you do not deceive; it necessitates that you keep your promises to others and to yourself, no matter how small.

7) Being kind to people enhances peace. Performing good deeds, community service, and doing your part to make the world a better place will reinforce positive beliefs, and so, your personal inner peace and sense of meaning.

8) Keeping your life in perspective enhances peace. No matter what you do, or who you are, in the human sense, you will certainly be gone in a blink of the sun's life.

9) The meaning of each person's life is for him or her to decide.

10) The material world has nothing to do with your inner peace. Your inner peace comes from within you.

And consider the following for thought...

11) If you take yourself too seriously, you may find yourself constantly looking for answers, without stopping to enjoy the happiness inherent in the answers you have already found.

12) Choose to enjoy yourself rather than to endure yourself. Being you is the only way in which you will experience the universe. You will be with yourself for your entire existence.

13) Live life without secrets. This way you will be free from fear that your secrets will be used against you.

14) Live a life of compassion toward all that lives. Doing so will minimize your suffering.

15) Measure your achievements against your potential, do not measure them against the achievements of others.

16) Only you are able to measure your success in life. Everyone measures success differently.

17) All people can be enlightened about the deep inner peace which they can possess. You can enlighten others by the example of your life.

Other Reading

I have learned a great deal from reading religious texts. I have also learned a great deal from the writings of many authors and philosophers. Some books which are more accessible include *A History of God* by Karen Armstrong, Ballantine Books (1994); *The Power of Myth* by Joseph Campbell (with Bill Moyers), Anchor (1991); *Sophie's World* by Jostein Gaarder, Paulette Moller (translator), Boulevard (1996); *Freedom of Choice Affirmed* by Carliss Lamont, Continuum (1990); *Cosmos*, and also, *The Dragons of Eden* by Carl Sagan, Ballantine Books (1993 and 1989, respectively).

A few books which are a bit less accessible are *Relativity* by Albert Einstein, Robert W. Lawson (translator), Outlet (1988); *A Brief History of Time* by Stephen Hawking, Bantam Doubleday Dell (1998); *The Age of Reason* by Thomas Paine, Prometheus Books (1985); *The Problems of Philosophy* by Bertrand Russell, Oxford University Press (1998); *A Guide for the Perplexed* by E.F. Schumacher, HarperCollins (1978); *The Passion of the Western Mind* by Richard Tarnas, Ballantine Books (1993); and *Consilience* by Edward Wilson, Knopf (1998).

About the Author

David Naggar is an attorney, entrepreneur, and author. He graduated Phi Beta Kappa from the University of California, Berkeley, and received his Juris Doctor from the Boalt Hall School of Law in 1981. For over twenty years, Mr. Naggar has passionately studied his avocation: humanity's search for answers to the deeper questions of life. Mr. Naggar is also the author of the book *The Music Business (Explained in Plain English)*. He lives in San Francisco, California.